# ANTIGONE PROJECT: A PLAY IN 5 PARTS

conceived by Chiori Miyagawa and Sabrina Peck

*Hang Ten by Karen Hartman*

*Medallion by Tanya Barfield*

*Antigone Arkhe by Caridad Svich*

*A Stone's Throw by Lynn Nottage*

*Red Again by Chiori Miyagawa*

<u>NoPassport Press</u>

Dreaming the Americas Series

## Antigone Project

**NoPassport Press, Dreaming the Americas Series**

First edition 2009 by NoPassport Press, ISBN: 978-0-578-03150-7;

PO Box 1786, South Gate, CA 90280 USA; -
NoPassportPress@aol.com, $20.00

# contents

## ACKNOWLEDGEMENTS

The play was conceived by Sabrina Peck and Chiori Miyagawa and commissioned by Crossing Jamaica Avenue with the support of Puffin Foundation. In different stages of the project, we received developmental support from various theaters: Second Stage, Classical Stage Company, and The Public Theater's NEW WORKS NOW! These readings were directed by Sabrina Peck. The final production at Women's Project was made possible, in part, by Sabrina Peck and Crossing Jamaica Avenue.

*Antigone Project* opened at Women's Project in October 2004, directed by Annie Dorsen (*Antigone Arkhe*), Dana Harrel (*Medallion*), Anne Kaufman (*Hang Ten*), Barbara Rubin (*Red Again*) and Lisel Tommy (*A Stone's Throw*), with the cast of Tracie Thoms, Jeanine Serralles, Joey Collins, April Yvette Thompson, Angel Desai, and Desean Terry.

Amy Yoshitsu was the Format Editor for this edition.

# Preface

## O Antigone

Imagine a relay race, but there is only one runner.

O Antigone. Try to grasp her.

Antigone. With a baton of justice in her hand, she runs, runs.

She must bury her brother Polynices, killed at the hand of their other brother, Eteocles, but it is against the law. The newly appointed King Creon forbids it, because Polynices fought on the wrong side in Thebes' civil war. His punishment is a form of familial torture and shame: they leave his body to be devoured and defaced by wild animals, a form of going to hell. Antigone must sanctify her brother's body by giving him a proper burial. Now, with the law and fate against her, like her father, Oedipus before her, she must heed her own moral code. She must act in time and against time, and will set off a series of tragedies and betrayals in the process. Haimon will stand up to his father in defense of Antigone, his fiancé. Antigone's sister Ismene will try to take responsibility for her actions. Eurydice will lose her son Haimon to suicide and then kill herself. King Creon will lose everyone. If it sounds like a Texas soap opera or a Greek tragedy, it is because it is.

Imagine this is a theatrical relay through time and space, in which Antigone's narrative is passed from writer to writer, as it is in the *Antigone Project*. The brainchild of Chiori Miyagawa and Sabrina Peck at Crossing Jamaica Avenue, *Antigone Project* was written in response to the Patriot Act signed into law on October 26, 2001. Karen Hartman, Tanya Barfield, Caridad Svich, Lynn Nottage, signed on to portray Antigone in a kaleidoscope of historic periods to see how she fares. Antigone's desperate striving towards sanctity, justice and rest (a step towards peace) are amplified by the hysteria of the post 9-11 Bush war on terror.

The clock is ticking, because of course, as in all races, Olympian and mortal, the race is against time, which is running out.

Bam.

You are off.

*Antigone Project* sets out at a sprint in Karen Hartman's contemporary arrhythmic and rhythmic erotic dialogue in her piece, *Hang Ten.*

The sounds of water are made by tongues and teeth, and Haemon disguised as the *otoosexy* surfer boy rises in a tide of corporeal images, like, well, like a Greek god, *a kouros* from the waves, sparking both Ismene's and Antigone's desires. Of course they're hot for him, with his jams taut at his hipbones, its laces begging to be tugged. Surfer boy is hot but, we will learn, he has no power. It's his very youth that reminds us, the public, that this mythic family is already caught in the entropic vortex of war, that, blinded and dead, has already taken most of the family down.

So we spin into *Medallion*, Tanya Barfield's 1918 vision of Antoinette a black laundress, who, to the sounds of stenographers transcribing condolence letters, demands, with stubborn and dignified beauty, some kind of Medal of Honor in lieu of her missing brother's body.

"Colored boys got a way of disappearing" She says to the white officer who refuses to give anything but the truly tragic answer, "True. It is a pity."

In Caridad Svich's *Antigone Arkhe*, an archivist uses the documents and artifacts unearthed in an archeological dig, to beautifully reconstruct

Antigone's narrative and the rituals inherent in the journey of the body: it's quest for love, it's longing for immortality, and the ultimate lament for its own lost life. The piece is an elegy and dirge to Antigone's known fate, which all of us, including Antigone herself, are aware. But in a dramatic reversal the writer veers away from Sophocles version of the myth and allows Antigone to take her death into her own hands. Lynn Nottage's piece, *A Stone's Throw*, recalls the disproportionate punishment of women in various religions, countries, and political climates, for breaking unreasonable laws. The play opens with the punishment and twirls back through time to show how, Antigone's simple love and sound morality ultimately conflict with the societal code and the laws and inevitably lead her astray. We witness her as she asks her sister to assure her daughter that she has actually done nothing wrong, while we know, that her death will not be merely her own. Finally, in Chiori Miyagawa's *Red Again*, Antigone and Harold (Haemon) re-meet in the underworld because as Harold says, " We didn't get to finish our story."

In a kind of time-warp aria, the piece invokes some of the injustices caused by political conflict worldwide, and Harold and Antigone cannot agree on right action. Antigone accuses Harold of meditating too much, while Harold finds Antigone full of rage. Irene reports on and gives perspective on the world situation. Only which world is it? Iraq, Saigon, New York? As the *Antigone Project*'s last play comes to a close, Irene reminds us of the very specific Greek way of seeing tragedy and its endless cycles of familial violence. Irene reminds us that Antigone will always be here to remind us.

This collection of plays confirms that Antigone as a metaphor continues to be contemporary and relevant. Dead in her cave, it's hard not to think of Antigone as a Christ-figure, possibly rising. In all of the plays there is a motif of rising. Rising from the dead, rising out of the ashes. While we know from Sophocles's original narrative she won't, the playwrights let Antigone's destiny remain open to interpretation, to wonder, to the imagination. Tragedy no longer has just one ending. *Antigone Project* demands we revisit her myth in light of our present circumstances. It also reminds us that to seek justice requires vigilance, constant renewal of the spirit, and the willingness to see anew. It beckons us to rise out of the current of history and re-envision so that we may create new possibilities, new hope.

While *Antigone Project* was conceived immediately in the wake of 9-11, I write this preface in the first weeks of 2009, almost eight years after the project has begun. The five Antigone plays remind us of the ceaselessness of political conflict in the middle east, specifically, the now (seemingly) endless war in Iraq and, of course, of the disastrous Israeli Palestinian conflict. In the wake of these atrocities, Antigone rises. She demands we remember every family member, unjustly killed. And every body, not recovered, every body that cannot receive its proper burial, still unburied. By the time you read this, we as a nation might have collectively forgotten the hundreds of unjust civilian casualties this week, or last week or last year. But Antigone will always remember. Follow her. Her moral code, her sacrifice, at the very least, will always remind us of what we are willing to risk, of what we are willing to sacrifice, of our very selves, if we dare to listen.

--Lisa Schlesinger

# Introduction

## Antigone Across Time

Ancient dramatic texts must always be recreated for modern audiences. The myths are eternal, but they can reappear in fresh ways. As T.S Eliot said:

> We shall not cease from exploration,
>
> And the end of all our exploring
>
> Will be to arrive where we started
>
> And know the place for the first time.
>
> Where the last of earth left to discover
>
> Is that which was the beginning. (Little Gidding)

This way every audience comes to "know the place for the first time" and learn something new, not only about the beauty of the ancient myths, but about themselves and the modern world.

Antigone may be the first freedom fighter in western literature. She has always inspired playwrights, and plays about her confrontation with organized government have been used to protest against oppressive regimes: Athol

Fugard's *1973* version of *Antigone* (*The Island*) indicts apartheid in South Africa as black prisoners perform the play on Robben Island, where many were detained indefinitely for opposing the racist system. Nelson Mandela played Creon in that same prison system. In 1984 four versions of *Antigone* were produced in Ireland to condemn colonial occupation.[1]

*Antigone* (ca. 441 BC) by the ancient Greek playwright Sophocles is based on a myth that goes back at least to Homer (8th century BC). Antigone is the daughter of Oedipus who killed his father and married his mother, but would not rest until he discovered the truth about himself. Antigone is truly his daughter, and once she decides to defend what she knows is right, that "unwritten law of the gods," she will not waver.

Sophocles' *Antigone* celebrates the first heroine in the full sense of the word. She insists on burying her brother who was killed in a civil war, even though Creon, the king of Thebes, had forbidden it. Antigone is the first conscientious objector, opposing the king, and what she sees as his unjust laws. Heroine though she may be, Antigone's confrontation with Creon is not

---

[1] See *Amid Our Troubles: Irish Versions of Greek Tragedy*, ed. Marianne McDonald and J. Michael Walton (London: Methuen, 2002).

necessarily clear-cut. There are many conflicting interpretations of this play. The early nineteenth century German philosopher Friedrich Hegel, who claimed it was the finest play ever written, saw two legitimate rights in opposition: the right of the family against the rights of the state. Familial values conflict with state interests, and the duty towards the gods of the underworld is opposed to the duty of obeying the ruler, whose rights are sanctioned by the Olympian gods. Personal issues confront public issues, and they radically confront each other.

More than an opposition of rights, however, the original play brilliantly shows us the opposition of two passionate people (Creon and Antigone) who go hell-bent to their own destruction. Antigone's hot-headedness is particularly clear in a couple of brutal exchanges with her sister. Nevertheless she is indisputably a heroine who knows her duty to her family.

Creon tries to be the best ruler he can be and to benefit the city in the aftermath of a bitter civil war. There were precedents in ancient Greece for not burying the body of one's enemy, but Sophocles questions such a course of action. Antigone is also right to honor the proper burial that the gods of the underworld demand. Both should have compromised, but neither did. That's why we have a tragedy.

Creon opposes Antigone with the might of law on which he says personal happiness is based, namely through a well-controlled city. With Sophocles' usual dramatic economy, Antigone is punished by the ruler whose laws she opposes, and Creon is punished by the loss of his own family, whose values he subordinated to those of the city.

The choral interludes in this play speak of all that concerns man: victory, defeat, life, death, love, hate, crime and punishment. As usual, Greek tragedy gives us insight into ourselves and asks questions.

Some modern commentators see right only in Antigone, and view Creon as a stereotypical dictator in the wrong. Bertolt Brecht blackened Creon with fascist colors; and Ireland's Tom Paulin presented Creon with the same strident rhetoric as the bigoted Northern Irish Protestant leader Ian Paisley. However, things are not so simple in Sophocles' play. Anouilh wrote one play on *Antigone* to be performed during the Nazi occupation of France that shows a reasonable Creon, and a rather silly adolescent-minded Antigone, but he is still ultimately on the side of Antigone.

Whereas these are all plays written by men, and interpreted by men, what distinguishes the five plays in *Antigone Project* is that women are defining the major issues. These multi-racial women playwrights are reclaiming Antigone for themselves and allowing fresh voices to interpret the myth that supplies the syntax behind their words. These authors take the Antigone story out of the patriarchal Greek setting and bring it into the new society in which a woman can run for president or vice-president.

The original performance of *Antigone Project* was in 2004 as a co-production between The Women's Project and Crossing Jamaica Avenue at the Julia Miles Theatre in New York. Each of the five parts that comprise the project lasts about fifteen minutes, so the five total about seventy-five minutes, about the same performance length of the usual ancient tragedy. Each reflects the author's special concerns. Each part had different women directing.

*Hang Ten*, by Karen Hartman, features a surfing culture with attractive young women in their thirties. They bemoan the ruler, Creon (obviously the head of an oppressive regime), although the play is never so specific. Antigone shows compassion for the boys' surfing, but is critical of the culture that produces such surfers and she dreads an accident. Ismene sees everything in a positive light. This contrast also existed in Sophocles' play. Ismene represents the complacent majority.

Following the myth, the siblings are Antigone, Ismene, Polynices, Eteocles and Oedipus, all children of Jocasta (since Oedipus is the father of the previous four, the incest is obvious). There's a cute joke about the father locking the kids out as he looks at "incest flicks."

Antigone announces she will bury their brother. It seems there was a conflict between two sides of the family, and now his burial is forbidden.  Ismene warns "We're under surveillance," another modern allusion, which could apply not only to America, but also to any country subject to oppressive control.

Antigone makes the speech:

That kid tips over and another pops up. You employ a surfer, he finds a real girlfriend, and a new boy comes to work. I get married and if after seven years or fourteen or twenty-one the guy absconds keels over, I replace him....Birth a kid, kid drowns in the bath, birth another. ....To make a new brother, I'd have to make a new me.

Those who know *Antigone* would recognize this speech as a reworking of the heroine's claim that she would not do what she did for a husband or a child, but only for a brother, arguing that the former are replaceable; since her mother and father are dead, a brother is irreplaceable (p. 37).[2]

A surfer (who turns out to be Haemon) appears and pledges love to Antigone. Then he asks which one is Antigone. Ismene says she is (Antigone), and she accepts the boy's offer. This shows that this Haemon, Creon's son, is interested more in doing the acceptable thing, just like Ismene. Here he's more of a conformist than the rebel he was in the original.

One is left with a bleak feeling as the rest of the "virtual" play may unfold, following the myth, with disaster for Antigone, but "the rest is silence." This play will be much richer for an audience familiar with the original story of Antigone.

*Medallion* by Tanya Barfield is much more straightforward. Antigone here is asking that her brother who fought heroically in World War I be given a medal and recognition for what he did. She also asks for his body back. It is made clear from the beginning that Americans do not honor their blacks. "Antoinette," our Antigone stand-in, meets with bureaucratic stonewalling from the Creon in this play, Carlton, who boasts about the

---

[2] All references to and translations of the original are from Sophocles' *Antigone*, trans. Marianne McDonald (2004; rpt. London: Nick Hern Books, 2000).

heroes in his family, whom we all know received honors, from burial as a hero to a medal, because they were white. Antoinette is told "Mrs. Thebes, the French may award Croix de Guerre to the Negroes, but we do not." Antoinette is finally dismissed and silenced by Carlton turning on a radio. This is a moving play about racial injustice.

*Antigone Arkhe* by Caridad Svich is a meta-theatrical piece, very interested in fragments from the past and how they are used. It uses lots of projections and technical aids and is by far the longest of all the pieces in performance time. The words dance with the projections, offering the commentary of a Greek chorus. Digital Antigone announces in a fragment that Antigone buried her brother's body, but the context is not elucidated. The "Narration" voice joins an Archivist, who speaks colloquially, and who describes an exhibit of various "things" ("a belt of hemp," presumably that Antigone used to kill herself) and body parts, including "A leg torn from a body." There is a statue that is filled out by the Digital Antigone, and a Historical Antigone speaks, longing for death and martyrdom as a way of accusing someone who has violated the laws of heaven. We are told Uncle Creon put his niece in a cave where she hung herself. At one point the Historical Antigone speaks about the process of recording her ("What? Talk into the machine?"), another metatheatrical element. A possible malfunction is discussed. Antigone herself seems to be the Ur-malfunction in a "civilized state." Antigone becomes a legend with her death.

Words from the first Chorus in Sophocles's play are cited "Beam of the sun, Eye of Golden Day," and a paraphrase of Creon's comment: "Remember this: our country is the ship that bears us safe, and that only if she thrives in her voyage can we make honest friends." The originals of these paraphrases are:

> First ray of sun, fairer than any seen before
>
> By Thebes of the seven gates,
>
> At last you appear,
>
> Golden eye of day
>
> Glancing over the streams of Dirce….(p. 7).

And Creon's: "I know our salvation is the ship of state and only those who keep her on the right course can be called her friends and benefactors" (p. 9).

It is interesting that the Archivist describes "A wedding dress from the Hellenistic period," a period which is at least a century later than Sophocles' *Antigone,* and several centuries later than the mythical Antigone. Perhaps this is a commentary on how Antigone has survived throughout the ages in a fragmentary form.

Antigone's body in this play is said to move from place to place, finally to be frozen in time. The body-parts (a finger and an eye), illustrate the fragmentation of the myth. The Historical Antigone and the Digital Antigone hang themselves for the audience's benefit, yet they continue to speak. The myth suddenly becomes a ghost. It is said that her body and brain have been preserved. The outcome is that she has become the physical reification of the myth in a museum, and the Archivist asks for financial support: now the myth has become a commercial product. The corpse is shown in the final scene as the doors of the palace open. This is the last ironic commentary, the ultimate capitalist triumph, in which, it seems, the imagination is dead. Do these plays themselves sell? Svich's play aptly shows how the myth has been perverted and Antigone has become the ultimate trophy wife of modernity.

Lynn Nottage's play, ominously entitled *A Stone's Throw*, is set in Africa and in a village where a woman is being stoned to death for an illicit affair with a man, even if he had promised to marry her, and had abandoned her after making her pregnant. It begins with the ending, the execution of a woman buried in sand up to her neck. She is about to be stoned. She suddenly remembers the time when they both said "I like you."

A flashback follows. This Antigone discusses her situation with Ismene as they pound grain. Ismene warns her. Then another flashback as the gentle seduction unfolds gradually. The man offers to wait a year, and bring a dowry then (she is widowed, but he must still bring a dowry to her father to win him over to his proposal). He offers to leave, but she tells him her name, Antigone, and he asks why she did that...and then they exchange the "I like you" phrase we heard at the beginning. They kiss passionately and we are back hearing the accusations of the reporters that we heard at the beginning as they accuse her and take pictures.

This ring composition is effective, besides showing a feisty Antigone following her heart in passionate rebellion against the state as she tells Creon: "I was born to love, not to hate." This play is an excellent illustration of how injustice still operates against women. Caridad Svich's play showed the theoretical underpinning of the myth; the play adapts it to a story that moves our hearts as much as Sophocles' play did for the abuse and suffering of this young woman.

*Red Again* by Chiori Miyagawa also touches the heart. It is very political much as is *Medallion*, because it deals with racial and ethnic prejudice, in addition to the other themes that are found in the original Sophoclean *Antigone*. The play is set clearly in the present, with a vivid memory of recent atrocities. Here we have an Asian, and specifically Japanese, perspective that incorporates beliefs from Buddhism. It's rather like a Zen *No Exit*, but here an exit is offered through reincarnation: "Red Again." Unlike the hero and heroines in Jean-Paul Sartre's 1944 play set in the underworld, these people in *bardo* (the Tibetan Buddhist transition chamber between death and a new life) will not be condemned to rehearse their mistakes for eternity, if indeed they learn the lessons offered from their past lives. Nevertheless, in both plays the characters look at their past life, and hear the people left on earth, and both are impelled by an existentialist drive to define themselves in spite of the absurdity of the world they face. Neither of them suffers from anything so crude as "hell fire," or physical torture.

Antigone broke the law by defying the "king," and attempting to bury her brother. Her brother here was innocent of any crime, but a victim of racial profiling: police officers misconstrued his wallet for a gun. Haemon, here called Harold, followed her because he thought she would suffer without him. He is more interested in meditating than fighting.

Antigone was protesting against the abuses of the world and the new police state under which they were constantly under surveillance (clearly Bush's

America after 9/11/2001). Each has different approaches to the world: Harold thinks the world can be changed through meditation, whereas Antigone opts for defiance and revolution. She now chooses to "honor her ancestors" and her "traditions"; this is a Japanese twist to "honoring the unwritten laws of the gods," as the Sophoclean Antigone did.

Irene (the Ismene figure) knows about the abuses, including the Japanese in America in concentration camps during World War II, besides the horror of Hiroshima and Nagasaki with Americans dropping atomic bombs that targeted civilians. Then she cites Treblinka (an infamous Nazi concentration camp in Poland), together with the racial atrocities of Bosnia and Cambodia. Irene, whose name means peace in Greek, defends peace at any price and does not defy the law in the way Antigone does. She recites the problems of their family's incestuous origin, a father "who gouged his eyes out for his crimes of unnatural sex and parricide" and two brothers, named Eteocles and Polynices, killing each other. The reasons are not given.

In the *bardo* waiting room, they have books that tell them about themselves, books of fate and human effort, and blank ones for the future. Antigone reads about one friend who left her comfortable bourgeois house to strike out on her own, like Ibsen's Nora, in his 1879 *Dolls House,* or Miss Helen in Fugard's 1984 *Road to Mecca.* Her name is Kate. Is this the shrew that left after taming?

Perhaps Antigone's lesson is that she should not be so much of a madwoman, as Irene pointed out, although she can still defend human rights, and perhaps Harold will learn compassion and humanity towards others even while meditating and in a convent: both are convinced they will find each other in their new lives. This is a love story about two admirable people, and it ends with more hope than any of the plays in this project about Antigone: like Buddhism, it allows learning from one's mistakes and giving those in error another chance.

To quote the Sophoclean original:

There are many wonders in the world,

But nothing more amazing than man!

And in this case that 'man' is a 'woman.' These new plays celebrate the potential of women to achieve glory, not in winning wars, but in following their conscience. They also show us victims, but at least all of them followed their passionate dreams.

Should we take a stand as Antigone does when we see clearly that something is wrong? Or should we choose Ismene's part, and follow the leader? Will no one ever learn the lessons from their past, and how compromise benefits both cities and individuals? That choice of what to do is always yours.

Marianne McDonald, Ph.D., MRIA

Professor of
Theatre and Classics

University of
California, San Diego

# ANTIGONE PROJECT

Historical Antigone (Jeanine Serralles) in *Antigone Arkhe* by Caridad Svich, Directed by Annie Dorsen @ The Women's Project, 2004. Photo: T. Charles Erickson.

# CAST OF CHARACTERS

## Suggested Breakdown

Actor 1 (Female, African American): Antigone in *Stone's Throw*; Irene in *Red Again*

Actor 2 (Female): Ismene in *Hang Ten*; Historical Antigone in *Antigone Arke*; Reporter in *Stone's Throw*

Actor 3 (Male, Caucasian): Carlton in *Medallion*; Archivist in *Antigone Arke*; Judge/Reporter in *Stone's Throw*; Harold in *Red Again*

Actor 4 (Female, African American) : *Antoinette in Medallion*; Narrator in *Antigone Arke*; Ismene in *Stone's Throw*

Actor 5 (Female): Antigone in *Hang Ten*; Reporter in *Stone's Throw*; Antigone in *Red Again*

Actor 6 (Male, African American) Surfer in *Hang Ten*; Man in *Stone's Throw*

# ANTIGONE PROJECT: A PLAY IN 5 PARTS

## conceived by Chiori Miyagawa and Sabrina Peck

## HANG TEN

### by Karen Hartman

## MEDALLION

### by Tanya Barfield

## ANTIGONE ARKHE

### by Caridad Svich

## A STONE'S THROW

### by Lynn Nottage

## RED AGAIN

### by Chiori Miyagawa

# HANG TEN
## by Karen Hartman

*ANTIGONE AND ISMENE WATCH THE WAVES. GOOD-LOOKING WOMEN IN THEIR THIRTIES. THEY MAKE SOFT WAVE-CRASHING SOUNDS WITH THEIR MOUTHS.*

ISMENE: I ride that one.

ANTIGONE: I ride that one.

ISMENE: Watch it break.

ANTIGONE: How can you say break when my heart is breaking?

ISMENE: Breakers break. It's a term.

ANTIGONE: How long a term?

ISMENE: Creon is king for life.

ANTIGONE: So, not that long.

ISMENE: I'll ride that one.

ANTIGONE: See the seal?

ISMENE: It's a boy.

ANTIGONE: It's a creature.

ISMENE: A boy is a creature. He's standing. He's riding his board.

*THE WOMEN WATCH THE BOY RIDE HIS BOARD.*

ANTIGONE: I can't look.

ISMENE: Look. Beauty heals.

ANTIGONE: I can't watch another boy fall.

ISMENE: It's sport.

ANTIGONE: It's sick. He tries with all his might, He works his pecs in his mom's garage, he pumps iron from a catalogue so he hold up the board, paddle out, paddle paddle. He goes to a beach where he knows no one: he kneels, he bites it, he kneels, he holds it, he stands, he bites it, he stands, he holds it, he stands, he stands, he stands. He's ready to come to his home beach and ride waves in front of us, in front of girls –

ISMENE: We're not his demographic.

ANTIGONE: – in front of babes –

ISMENE: We're twice his age.

ANTIGONE: He gets hard little muscles down his skinny front, saves up for a springsuit, the neoprene binds his biceps and thighs, he powders his body so the little hairs won't stick, so he can zip up a size too small, an armor of latex against the shrivelly cold sea. He dreams of riding water. Now peak of summer, thirty-one shades of blue, suit peeled back to show fourteen karat skin, he hefts a waxed longboard into ocean from here to Hawaii. Save for the braces on his teeth he is a buttfuckable Hellenic god. He plunges. He paddles. He rides. But how will it end? How does it end no matter how worthy, how pretty, how ready the boy? Waves crash one way, into coast, into rock. I can't look.

*ANTIGONE HAS BEEN LOOKING THIS WHOLE TIME.*

ISMENE: Antigone. You're an ass. The coast is soft. Sand. The kid can swim. You know this. You're an ass.

ANTIGONE: Did we have the same brother or not?

ISMENE: Brothers.

ANTIGONE: One day riding the wet, the next sucked under the ground.

ISMENE: That kid is somebody else.

ANTIGONE: Same youth rising into my hand.

ISMENE: Keep it to yourself.

ANTIGONE: Same stubble under my tongue.

ISMENE: Think of the family.

ANTIGONE: "Family?" You mean you?

ISMENE: I guess so.

ANTIGONE: It's terrifying that we are blood.

ISMENE: Sure is.

ANTIGONE: Same brothers, same father. Three brothers if you count our father. Jocasta must have been so proud of her kids: Antigone, Ismene, Polynices, Eteoclos, Oedipus.

ISMENE: That's the part you could leave out.

ANTIGONE: Incest is efficient.

ISMENE: That's the kind of sentence you could write down and leave under a rock. On a different beach.

ANTIGONE: Incest, invest: a philosophy. Invest in what you already know.

ISMENE: There once was a girl names Ismene. She had parents and siblings. They were not the same people. She was an exiled princess surviving a war. Her brothers fought on different sides. That's okay. Families split and that is okay. That is how humans move on, the capacity to love new people. The rules changed. The ruler changed. And everyone forgot about Princess Ismene's rotten family. Such that she got a really good job with Full benefits and two-hour lunches in a seaside

ISMENE (Cont): town and watched surfers all afternoon. She hired the surfers to do odd jobs for her, washing walks or clipping flora. They wear little pants called jams. These jams expose the hipbones and unlace below the navel. Ismene was a lucky lucky princess.

ANTIGONE: I'm burying our brother.

ISMENE: Make a shrine. It's portable.

ANTIGONE: I want the body.

ISMENE: Show some respect for boundaries.

ANTIGONE: Boundaries are for cowards.

ISMENE: There's the reason four of six of us are dead.

ANTIGONE: I'm crossing back for him.

ISMENE: No him anymore. It. A body is an it.

*ANTIGONE LOOKS OUT TO SEA.*

ANTIGONE: Where did the boy go?

ISMENE: Swimming.

ANTIGONE: Sucked down.

ISMENE: Watch your language.

ANTIGONE: I meant the sea.

ISMENE: He was my brother too.

ANTIGONE: What color were that surfer boy's jams?

ISMENE: I didn't see.

ANTIGONE: The wrong color?

ISMENE: I didn't see.

ANTIGONE: He was right there.
Let's go in.

ISMENE: We're under surveillance.

ANTIGONE: So?

ISMENE: *(OUT TO SEA)* Look there.

ANTIGONE: Oh.

ISMENE: See?

ANTIGONE: Is that the same one?

ISMENE: Sure.

ANTIGONE: I like that one.

ISMENE: See?

ANTIGONE: I don't think it's the same.

ISMENE: But you like that one.

ANTIGONE: Yes.

ISMENE: Enjoy.

ANTIGONE: I need a fresh beverage.

ISMENE: Tough.

ANTIGONE: I'd like a little more freedom of motion.

ISMENE: We earn that. When we're really good. We earn that.

ANTIGONE: I will earn freedom through death!

ISMENE: Here.

*SHE HANDS ANTIGONE BINOCULARS.*

ANTIGONE: You were hoarding this whole time?

ISMENE: Saving.  You first.

ANTIGONE: Thanks, sis.

*ANTIGONE WATCHES THE BOY THROUGH
BINOCULARS.  SHE GASPS IN PLEASURE.*

ISMENE: Good?

ANTIGONE: Uh huh.

ISMENE: What can you see?

ANTIGONE: Every swell.  Every drop.  He sets his
face against the waves.  He squints.  He likes the
challenge.  He's in Creon's colors.

ISMENE: Good.

ANTIGONE: He's got a sharktooth around his neck.

ISMENE: Cute.

ANTIGONE: The spike of it coated with blood.

*ANTIGONE SETS DOWN THE BINOCULARS.*

ISMENE: You don't like that one?

ANTIGONE: I want my brother.

ISMENE: Boys spring fresh from the waves every day.

ANTIGONE:  That kid tips over and another pops up. You employ a surfer, he finds a real girlfriend, and a new boy comes to work. I get married and if after seven years or fourteen or twenty-one the guy absconds keels over, I replace him. An equivalent model or a full shift – a teenager, a woman, whatever. Birth a kid, kid drowns in the bath, birth another. Too late, get one from an economically deprived nation. Gulp down a drink, there's free refills.

ANTIGONE (Cont): To make a new brother I'd have to make a new me. We would sit and go, I think dad locked us out of the house to watch porn. Did that happen? We would reflect and confirm.

ISMENE: He became a traitor. He fought against everything that keeps us safe.

ANTIGONE: "Safe?"

ISMENE: I loved him too.

ANTIGONE: You have no loyalty.

ISMENE: I am loyal to change.

ANTIGONE: You mean convenience?

ISMENE: Get married.

ANTIGONE: There is no one like a brother.

ISMENE: A sister?

ANTIGONE: I don't know, I never lost a sister.

ISMENE: *(OF DAD)* It was an incest flick.

ANTIGONE: How do you know?

ISMENE: I read the box. I'm older. I could read, I read the box.

ANTIGONE: We never talk about this stuff.

ISMENE: We could.

ANTIGONE: Polynices and I talked all night about this stuff.

ISMENE: Keep it to yourself.

ANTIGONE: I always thought there could be anything between us, me and him. But you and me? I never considered that.

ISMENE: I exist. I am right here and I have been right here this whole time. I hate my fucking family.

ANTIGONE: "Family?" You mean me?

ISMENE: You crash through the barbed wire with a bucket of sea water to slosh over our brother, who's left behind? Me. Are they going to freshen my drink? You see free refills here? They'll go, where's your sister? And I can say blood is nothing till I bleed through my shorts but they will hold me to you.

*ANTIGONE PREPARES FOR THE RITES. ULULATES.*

I'm going to get married and get pregnant and name my kids names that start with O, P, and E. I'm going to make a family tree. It will be messy, the branches sort of branching into branches instead of dividing into leaves... But that's okay. I'm not ashamed of my past. Okay I'm ashamed but I think that when I have the kids and a little security - my home is nice but ever since we've been invaded and placed under house arrest it's a lot less cozy - when I have security regarding this regime, when I line up my offspring with just the initials of those nasty people related to us, I'm going to feel soothed.

*A SURFER ENTERS. HE WEARS JAMS AND A BLOODY SHARKS' TOOTH NECKLACE. HE IS SOAKING WET.*

SURFER: I love you Antigone. I think you're rad. I have a plan for us Antigone. Creon is my dad. I am a prince and I love you. Some qualities I like in a girl are: the willingness to argue – most girls let me win because I'm the guy, and maybe the prince, but even just the guy – most girls let most guys win, they'll even switch sides, start arguing your side just because you were louder and maybe you scared them and maybe they fear violence, but it's lame. I hate girls who do that. Who are insipid and weak. I don't think girls should body build or anything but I believe in the goddess, an immortal courage that lies beneath the breast of many women, especially one that's a little older than me, not too old, not misshapen or flatulent but a little crinkled at the eye. That's cool. The chest above her bikini top a little rough, not leathery, just like: "I've seen some sun." I like that. I too have seen sun. I am young but I have seen much sun. I think about us sometimes Antigone. I think a woman as bold as you could be a lot of fun. I think we could do things. I'll say more on this subject when we know each other better. I think we could really really do things.

SURFER (Cont): I have a plan Antigone. What I'm going to do is explain to my father the politics of opposition movements, the necessity of preventing martyrdom. You are the ultimate martyr figure being a girl, or anyway female, and fighting for something people identify with. Fighting for family, which is a very feminine thing to do. You're fierce but like, fierce in the spirit of domesticity which is insanely appealing not only to women but men. And if you hang… I'll guarantee him there will be sea birds flocking around your ten toes. An ice plant wreath on your head. Little notes on sticks. Not only your bro's body but yours will be revered, people will cut threads from your tankini and frame them in their homes. You will turn the tides against us if you die. I'll explain this to my dad. And how if instead you love ME and I ALLOW you to do the deal with the corpse, if we make a bridge not a wall, you know, a bridge between regimes, Creon is your uncle, I am your cousin and I know in your family that should count for something, Hah hah.

Anyway. That's in the past. To me you are not tainted whatsoever.

Anyway. I think we'd be great. I think we'd be unbeatable.

Will you marry me Antigone?

SURFER (Cont): Which one is Antigone?

ISMENE: I am Antigone.  I'd love to.


*BLACKOUT.*

# MEDALLION
## by Tanya Barfield

*NOVEMBER 1918, A RAINY DAY.
ANTOINETTE, A BLACK LAUNDRY
WORKER, SITS IN THE OFFICE OF
GENERAL CARLTON.  SHE IS ALONE.
SHE HOLDS TWO TELEGRAMS AND A
SMALL SATCHEL.  THE SOUND OF
TELEPHONE OPERATORS AND
STENOGRAPHERS CAN BE HEARD.*

TELEPHONE OPERATOR: President Wilson issues address stop allies push back the German line stop.

STENOGRAPHER : Dear Mr. and Mrs. -- insert name, I write to offer sincere condolences.  Your son, -- insert, -- was killed, fighting at --insert...

*GENERAL CARLTON, A WHITE OFFICER,
ENTERS.  HE IS A WELL-EDUCATED, PRECISE,
ANGULAR MAN.  CARLTON GOES ABOUT HIS*

*BUSINESS: REMOVES HIS OVERCOAT, HANGS UP HIS UMBRELLA. HE SHAKES OFF A WET NEWSPAPER AS HIS BRIEFCASE SLIPS OUT OF HIS HANDS, ETC. HE DOES NOT SEE ANTOINETTE SITTING QUIETLY.*

TELEPHONE OPERATOR: Read by General Pershing to the French military mission stationed with the American Army -- Secret Information Concerning Black American Troops: It is important for French officers who have been called upon to exercise command over black American troops, to have an exact idea of the position occupied by Negroes in the United States...

STENOGRAPHER: Dear Mr. and Mrs. –

TELEPHONE OPERATOR: Although a citizen of the United States, the black man is regarded by the white American as an inferior being with whom relations of business or service only are possible.

STENOGRAPHER: Dear Mr. and Mrs. I write to offer sincere condolences.

TELEPHONE OPERATOR: We must not eat with blacks, must not shake hands or seek to talk or meet with them outside the requirements of military service. We must not commend too highly the black American troops, particularly in the presence of white Americans...

CARLTON WINDS A PHONOGRAPH. JAZZ MUSIC PLAYS. A SUDDEN BLAST OF HORNS AS HE TURNS AND SEES ANTOINETTE. COMPLETELY ALARMED, HE JUMPS BACK, GASPING.

ANTOINETTE: Give me my brother's body.

CARLTON QUICKLY SHUTS OFF THE RADIO.

CARLTON: I beg your pardon.

ANTOINETTE: Give me my brother's body.

CARLTON: Remove yourself from my office.

ANTOINETTE: The corpse.

CARLTON: Immediately.

*ANTOINETTE DOES NOT MOVE.*

If you do not remove yourself from my office, I will have you forcefully removed.

ANTOINETTE: My brother served in New York's 369th National Guard. He played in the regimental band.  He died at Champagne-Marne.  Please, give me his body.

CARLTON: Mrs.--?

ANTOINETTE: Antoinette Thebes—

CARLTON: Antoinette—

ANTOINETTE : General—

CARLTON: Carlton.

ANTOINETTE: *(HOLDING UP)* General Carlton. This schoolboy's satchel that was my brother's is empty. This bag to carry his breath, his skin. A bag for bones. Would you like t'see the contents of the satchel?

CARLTON: *(SOFTENING)* The bag is empty.

ANTOINETTE: Would you like to see?

CARLTON: Antoinette, you are feeling heartache. I know this feeling. I know the Negro man feels heartache as the white man does. And the woman has the same capacity for compassion and understanding as does the man. My beliefs may not be popular beliefs among my people. But I
CARLTON (Cont): believe they are just

beliefs.  And when men of the future observe history, it will stand on the side of clemency and temperance and not of rigor and restraint.   And this is why I will give you brief audience and not have you forcefully removed from my office.

ANTOINETTE: My brother's body...

CARLTON: Was unrecovered?

ANTOINETTE: Colored boys got a way of disappearing.

CARLTON: Pity.  True.  It is a pity.

*BEAT.*

But, we couldn't possibly identify -- and the expenditure of-

ANTOINETTE: Please. Sir. I want t'bury something of my brother.


CARLTON : An act of ritual. Important, I understand. Ritualistic acts are important even if they are based solely on imagination, or hopefulness -- a belief system that grants peace of mind.


ANTOINETTE: His name Paul Edward Thebes. IIe served New York's 369th National Guard Regiment, he died [in] Champagne-Marne.


CARLTON: Quite a battle.


ANTOINETTE: (*HOLDING UP A TELEGRAM.*) Telegram tells me he demonstrated exemplary courage. "Was Wounded. Saved a company of white boys. French award Medal of Honor. Have pride." This one from my other brother. "Paul killed (stop) will send home his ribbons and French medal (stop this) pray for us. " It never came.

CARLTON: The post can be—


ANTOINETTE: It never came.


CARLTON: We are at war, I sympathize, but—


ANTOINETTE : I need something t'bury.


CARLTON: A photograph, perhaps?


ANTOINETTE: General Carlton, I don't come from a family of clerks and stenographers. I come from a family of longshore and laundry workers. We don't got no photographs.


CARLTON: I'm sorry, I?


ANTOINETTE: Need a medal.


CARLTON: You've said yourself, the French medal was lost—

ANTOINETTE: From your government, from our government, this government, I need you to give me, you must give me, I need, and you must give, General Carlton you will give me a medal of honor—

CARLTON: A medal?

ANTOINETTE: For my brother.

CARLTON: Mrs. Thebes, the French may award Croix de Guerre to the Negroes, but we do not.

ANTOINETTE: Paul wounded Paul killed –

CARLTON: Stop—

ANTOINETTE: Squattin' in rotted rat-filled trenches, ears ripped by machine fire, burnt by shells, squalid smell of blood, knee deep in a wasted land of water

CARLTON: Stop it.

ANTOINETTE: Rats feedin' off the flesh of fresh cadavers,
eatin' the eyes, stealin' the sight

CARLTON: Antoi—

ANTOINETTE: Gassed for mother-land

CARLTON : An—

ANTOINETTE: Lost hand in battle –

CARLTON: Antoinette!

ANTOINETTE: Twisted and barbed by wire -- continued to fight.

CARLTON: I offer sincere condolences.

ANTOINETTE: You offer nothing!

CARLTON: Here you overstep yourself.

ANTOINETTE: You *must* give me a medal.

CARLTON: Here, Antoinette, you are entirely out of step.  I cannot possibly issue a medal of honor.

ANTOINETTE: A purple—

CARLTON: I cannot poss—

ANTOINETTE: A purp—

CARLTON: I have spoken and I have said.

ANTOINETTE: A purple medal—

CARLTON: Stop—

ANTOINETTE: My brother—

CARLTON: Stop it!

ANTOINETTE: My broth—

CARLTON: A purple heart is a medal.

ANTOINETTE: An organ.

CARLTON: A heart—

ANTOINETTE: An instrument—

CARLTON: Is a precious medal.

ANTOINETTE: For music.

CARLTON: I cannot possibly—

ANTOINETTE: Issue—

CARLTON: Any sort of medallion—

ANTOINETTE: Deliver—

CARLTON: A body—


ANTOINETTE: My brother—


CARLTON: A colored boy—


ANTOINETTE: To me.


CARLTON: Silence! I demand your silence now. I have been kind. I have been more than necessarily kind. Some men of my kind would not be so kind. And I demand your cessation in this matter. I demand you recognize your station and stay in step.


ANTOINETTE: My broth—

CARLTON: My father, a chaplain, died—


ANTOINETTE: My—


CARLTON: My youngest brother, a pilot died—

ANTOINETTE: My--


CARLTON: I cannot deliver a heart. Or a body. Or a medal. And you cannot come in to my office. You cannot come -- a Negro -- a black apparition—


ANTOINETTE: I must bury—


CARLTON: You must:


ANTOINETTE & CARLTON: Stop. You/I must bury—


CARLTON: A symbol?


ANTOINETTE : My brother's purple heart.

*THEY STARE AT EACH OTHER. CARLTON LOOKS AWAY FIRST. HE TURNS ON THE RADIO. MUSIC PLAYS.*

# ANTIGONE ARKHE

## by Caridad Svich


ARCHIVIST: An archive is a public building, a place where records are kept.

Archival memory may consist of documents, maps, literary texts, letters, archaeological remains, recordings, videos, films, cds, and other ephemera of society.


NARRATION: *In the blur of history*

*In the chaos of memory*

*Words are broken*
*Fragmented*
*Heard anew*


DIGITAL ANTIGONE: Antigone buried the body of her brother. False to him she will never be found.

ARCHIVIST: Thebes (now Thivai), chief city of Boeotia of ancient Greece. Here is the site of the Theban acropolis, part of which still survives. Here lie the remains of a prehistoric city.

Right here. Within this caverned rock, within this vault. In a chamber secret as a grave, she was held prisoner.


NARRATION: *The litany of the dead is borne here. Listen.*


HISTORICAL ANTIGONE: Punish me, brother.

Punish my love.

For I only loved, and my love costs me.

Your body rests, and my body is outside of me.

Your body rests, and I wrestle sleep.


ARCHIVIST: In this exhibit you will find

An ivory jewel-box

from a chamber tomb of Thebes.

A thin belt made of hemp

A simple dress made of silk

A leg torn from a body


HISTORICAL ANTIGONE: Awaking

the ever-new lament

In your death you have undone my life

The day-star's sacred eye watches me.

Oh city of my fathers in the land of Thebes.


ARCHIVIST: In this exhibit you will find

A statue of a young woman of about human size
from the Sanctuary on the mountain.

A mirror of undefined origin.

It was here. It was right here where they held her.
A caverned rock. A living tomb.

DIGITAL ANTIGONE: Antigone buried her brother. She carried his corpse for miles. She went against every law.

HISTORICAL ANTIGONE: Die I must. I know that well. Even without edicts. But if I am to die before my time, I count that as a gain: for when any one lives as I do, surrounded by evil, can such one find anything but gain in death? These times in which we live, these times of hate, have been lived before. I welcome death if it free me from these times, and from this well of hate. Accuse me of being Death's bride, and I will accuse you for centuries of going against the laws of heaven, which are beyond time. Make me your martyr. Your power is of this earth, and I am already in heaven.

SCROLL: *ANTIGONE IS LED AWAY BY THE GUARDS.*

NARRATION: *Out of earshot*

*Out of view*

*Her body quivers*

ARCHIVIST: In this exhibit you will find

A map of silence.

## Scene 2: Suspension

ARCHIVIST: She used a belt. A thin strap. She hung it from this point right here. You can see a mark where the rock juts out. She took the belt from around her waist and tied it around her neck, and suspended herself from this very point. She knew what she was doing when she spoke out. She buried her brother. That's not technically a crime, but the governor said it was forbidden. There are laws against treason and betrayal. She took his corpse, went out into the public field, buried him, and spoke over his grave, and sang a mournful song. She didn't sing quiet. She wanted the world to hear. So, she got put in here, shoved in like an animal. Creon locked the vault and thought nothing of it.

NARRATION: Antigone lets out a scream before she hangs.


ARCHIVIST: You can't hear anything in here except rain beating. Her uncle Creon put her in here. I think it's worst when it's a family thing. Uncles and brothers and sisters all mixed up in some political tangle…Yes. It was from this point she hung herself. …Why didn't they take away the belt?… what's a belt worth?…


HISTORICAL ANTIGONE & DIGITAL ANTIGONE: And then I/she stopped screaming, and wept instead, and tasted my/her tears, and tried to move but I/she was tired of wriggling; my/her body was spent. So I/she pretended to be a statue, like those I/she saw at the doors of the sanctuary.  I/She was trying to forget how to move. I/She was trying to forget how to speak. I/She was trying to forget how to weep. I/She was trying to forget.


ARCHIVIST: In this exhibit you will find

A thin belt made of hemp

A simple dress made of silk

And a lock of hair

## {Interlude: A private recording of Antigone

HISTORICAL ANTIGONE: …What? Talk into the machine? What do you mean? Closer? Okay. Is this close enough? …This feels funny. No, it's all right. I'll say things. I'll speak into it. I just don't want my voice to come out wrong. You know? It needs to sound like me. So that if someone were to pick it up and listen, they could say 'hey, that's Antigone. Hey, hey, that's not Johnny, no, that's Antigone"…What? You're recording me now? But I haven't…I'm not ready. I was just… You need a story, right? Something rich and wonderful. Isn't that what you want? Something about my father maybe? I lived with him in exile for years. I was his eyes. My father was a great man. He learned to forget his pride. That's the greatest lesson one could learn in this life…What? Oh. You don't want to hear about my father? …I can give you something else. What do you want? What do you want from me?}

ARCHIVIST: There seems to have been a malfunction.


HISTORICAL ANTIGONE (FROM RECORDING)

What do you -?


ARCHIVIST: There. There. It's over.

I'm sorry about that.

Machines have lives of their own sometimes.

Now, where were we? Ah yes. The belt around her neck. Silence.


DIGITAL ANTIGONE: *She was trying to forget how to move.*

*She was trying to forget how to speak.*
She was trying to forget.

ARCHIVIST: "She must die, and therefore serve the dead eternally, if that is her will." That's what he said. And he led her onto a lonely path, and hid her inside the rocky vault, with barely enough food to last a few days. He thought it the right thing to do. If she was hid, he would avoid public scandal. No one need know where Antigone was sent.

NARRATION: Antigone seeks her tomb. She wishes to be buried in her rightful place.

*"Where is my bridal chamber? Where is my gown?" she cries.*

DIGITAL ANTIGONE: I try to sleep but the siren sounds won't stop. Tighten the noose. Belly up close to thoughts coming in slow motion, suspended:

NARRATION: *Creon watches her from his study. He has the inside view.*

*She is his conscience. Best that she is locked up.*

*No one need hear her words of disobedience in this*
*civilized state.*

*In the vault she hangs*

*held inside a frame between marriage and death.*

ARCHIVIST: First second

DIGITAL ANTIGONE: Second second

NARRATION: Third…

ARCHIVIST: First second

NARRATION & ARCHIVIST: *Second second*

ARCHIVIST: Third…

HISTORICAL ANTIGONE: The belt cuts

into the neck

Slow torque

Feet kick once

Against rock

The eyes look up

The flow of oxygen throughout the body stops


SCROLL: *EXIT ANTIGONE ON THE SPECTATORS' LEFT.*


## Scene 3: Altar


SCROLL: *FROM THE CENTRAL DOORS OF THE PALACE.*


ARCHIVIST: An altar is placed for all to see.

Antigone is mourned.

Objects are left in her name upon the altar.

In this exhibit you will find

A pitcher of wine

A wooden amulet

The petal of dried rose


From this earth you will see

A lacerated neck

Bruised arms

Marks on the tongue

The stuff of legend.


NARRATION: *The litany of the dead is borne here.*
*Listen.*


DIGITAL ANTIGONE: Swung down

She fell upon the earth


HISTORICAL ANTIGONE: Seven hours later
they find me.

I am cut down, and laid out on the plain.


DIGITAL ANTIGONE: No more prison-locked is she

*THEY CRY*


NARRATION: *Beam of the sun*

*Eye of golden day*

*Remember this: our country is the ship that bears us safe, and that only if she thrives in her voyage can we make honest friends.*


ARCHIVIST: In this exhibit you will find

A wedding dress from the Hellenistic period

An abject copy of a death decree

A mirror

And a statue of a young woman

of about human size

HISTORICAL ANTIGONE: Here on warm earth stained with blood I walk

DIGITAL ANTIGONE: Under open sky breaking from the heat

HISTORICAL ANTIGONE: One step, and another

DIGITAL ANTIGONE: One girl, and another

HISTORICAL ANTIGONE: Each breath

DIGITAL ANTIGONE: Grants a little more…

HISTORICAL ANTIGONE: And as I look out

DIGITAL ANTIGONE: Beyond the plain,

across the open fields

HISTORICAL ANTIGONE: I hear the cries of the living

HISTORICAL ANTIGONE & DIGITAL ANTIGONE: And I touch the skirt of the river with my own bare hands.


## Scene 4: Statue


HISTORICAL ANTIGONE: While I rise

And when I rise

The voices of the dead call to me

And I listen

In exile

My body is transferred from Thebes

to another city

I watch it as it moves

As one city and another tries to make a place for it.

My body travels by ship,

And is frozen in time.

Someone wants a finger.

Someone else wants an eye.

Someone steals an eyelash in the night.


DIGITAL ANTIGONE: The tragedy of Antigone is played out on the stage.


ARCHIVIST: In this exhibit you will find

From this earth you will witness:


HISTORICAL ANTIGONE: A young woman
about the size of a statue


DIGITAL ANTIGONE: Held up for your scrutiny.


HISTORICAL ANTIGONE: Feel her pulse as she
wraps the belt around her neck.

Count the minutes it takes for the oxygen to leave
her body,


HISTORICAL ANTIGONE & DIGITAL
ANTIGONE: First second

Third second

Slow torque…


ARCHIVIST: What's your story, Antigone?


NARRATION
*In the blur of history*
*In the chaos of memory*

*Words are broken*

*Fragmented*

*Heard anew*


ARCHIVIST: Admit daylight

Admit error

Admit

Confess

Do not stand by ceremony

HISTORICAL ANTIGONE: And I crawl along the river lit by the moon.

DIGITAL ANTIGONE: And I crawl along the river lit by the moon.

NARRATION: *Where is her bridal chamber? Where is her wedding gown?*

DIGITAL ANTIGONE & HISTORICAL ANTIGONE: And I drink from the river.

NARRATION: *This is recalled*

*From another time*

DIGITAL ANTIGONE & HISTORICAL
ANTIGONE: I drink…


NARRATION: *Not long past*

DIGITAL ANTIGONE & HISTORICAL
ANTIGONE: While I rise

And when I rise

My statue breaks


ARCHIVIST: Antigone's body has been preserved forever. Her entire body including her brain has been preserved. Some recordings have also been found recently, and while the quality is not good, you can hear Antigone's voice in a special room next to the gift shop as you leave. You can also visit the archaeological museum, and delight in a prehistoric collection, a sculpture collection, a vase collection and a bronze collection from various sites and ancient cemeteries. The taking of photographs is strictly prohibited. A new extension to the museum is being planned, pending financial support. We welcome your contribution.

SCROLL: *THE DOORS OF THE PALACE ARE OPENED.*

*THE CORPSE OF ANTIGONE IS DISCLOSED.*

# A STONE'S THROW

## by Lynn Nottage

### Scene 1: The Execution

*A WOMAN IS BURIED UP TO HER HEAD IN DIRT. HER FACE IS COVERED WITH A WHITE SHROUD.*

ANTIGONE'S VOICE *(O.S. AMPLIFIED)* : I like you.

MAN'S VOICE *(O.S. AMPLIFIED):* I like you, too.

*THE WOMAN GASPS AT THE REMEMBRANCE.*

*BLACK OUT.*

## Scene 2: The Perp walk

*AN ORGY OF WHITE HOT FLASH BULBS.
ANTIGONE WALKS INCREDIBLY SLOWLY
ACROSS THE STAGE AS SHE'S BARRAGED BY A
CACOPHONY OF VOICES. SHE'S WEARING A
COLORFUL FLOWING BUBU.*

*THE ANTIGONE'S AGONY IS APPARENT IN
HER HEAVY LABORED STEPS. SHE
PROTECTIVELY PULLS A VEIL AROUND HER
MOUTH AND NOSE AS IF A FRIGHTENED
CHILD COWERING FROM A GROUP OF
BULLIES.*

A CHORUS OF REPORTERS VOICES (*O.S.
AMPLIFIED*): Did you?

Were you?

Are you aware of the law?

What would God say?

Did you?

Were you?

You are unmarried.


*SHE LIFTS HER ARMS TO PROTECT HERSELF
AND SILENCE THE REPORTERS.*


Do you respect the code of the law?

The law?

What about the law?

Heathen!


ANTIGONE: Stop.


*BLACK OUT.*


**Scene 3: The Trial**

*A LARGE VIDEO SCREEN DESCENDS.*

*WE SEE A YOUNG WOMAN NURSING A CHILD.*
*IT IS ANTIGONE, AND SHE SITS ERECT ON THE*
*WITNESS STAND. NERVOUS, TENTATIVE AND*
*RESIGNED.*

JUDGE *(O.S. AMPLIFIED):* How do you respond
to the accusations leveled against you?

ANTIGONE: Yes, I did it. I won't deny it. And,
I'm not ashamed. I will accept this punishment
alone, if no one else will stand beside me.

*AN ORGY OF WHITE HOT FLASH BULBS.*

*BLACK OUT.*

**Scene 4: The Confession**

*DAYLIGHT.*

*ISMENE AND ANTIGONE POUND GRAIN.*

*THE RHYTHM OF DAILY LIFE. ANTIGONE
STOPS. SHE PLACES HER HAND TO HER
MOUTH AND GASPS.*


ISMENE: What?


*ANTIGONE DECIDES AGAINST SPEAKING AND
RETURNS TO POUNDING GRAIN.*

*SHE STOPS AGAIN.*


ANTIGONE: Issie, no blood.


ISMENE: What?


ANTIGONE: *(LOUDER)* One moon.  No blood.


*THE WOMEN RETURN TO POUNDING GRAIN.*


Do you know what that means?

*HORRIFIED, ISMENE STOPS.*

ISMENE: It'll come tomorrow.

ANTIGONE: And if not tomorrow?

*ISMENE RETURNS TO POUNDING.*

ANTIGONE: Say something.

*ISMENE CONTINUES TO POUND.*

ANTIGONE: If not tomorrow?

*ISMENE STOPS POUNDING.*

ISMENE: Then when will it be plain?

ANTIGONE: Soon.  No, sooner.

*ISMENE GASPS, AND STRUGGLES TO HOLD
BACK TEARS.*

ANTIGONE: Please, don't--

ISMENE: You know--

ANTIGONE: Of course, I know.  I have no
husband.

ISMENE: God is merciful, but the law is not.

ANTIGONE: The law is vile and unforgiving, and
I don't respect it.

ISMENE: But it's there. And we women are
subject to the foolishness of men.

ANTIGONE: What can I do?

ISMENE: We'll say nothing. We'll do nothing. We'll finish what we're doing. We'll make fufu for dinner, we'll watch the sun set and we'll forget this.

ANTIGONE: Yes. We'll forget. Good.

*THEY RETURN TO POUNDING GRAIN.*

ISMENE: Does he know?

ANTIGONE: Yes.

ISMENE: And what did he say?

ANTIGONE: There was no witness to our love. He will carry no burden.

ISMENE: And you'll let him go unpunished?


ANTIGONE: I have no defense.


ISMENE: Feel this.


*ISMENE BALLS UP HER FIST.*


Feel it.


ANTIGONE: Why?


ISMENE: Feel it! This is the size, dirty stones pulled from a garden, they'll be large enough to hurt, but not kill immediately.   A hundred of them will slowly beat the life from you. Do you understand?

ANTIGONE: Yes, yes, yes…but I did nothing wrong. Nothing, do you understand? It wasn't wrong and you will tell my child this. Won't you?

ISMENE: No.  No.  Listen, I'll sell my sewing machine and mother's jewelry.  My husband knows people who can be persuaded.  We will persuade them to be forgiving.

ANTIGONE: It won't be enough! They're old men. And so they speak as if God. And there's no arguing.  You know that.

ISMENE: Well, I won't let you will die for a man who could offer you no dowry.

ANTIGONE: Issie, he carried my basket home from the crossroad. This man saw me struggling and carried a mule's load of groundnuts without knowing my name. Asked for nothing, other than I walk by his side. He'd seen me in the marketplace, and remembered what I wore on every Friday.  Even the pattern of that purple gelee cut from mother's wedding shawl. He bought nuts from only me, though you know I overcharge.  But he liked the way I roasted them. The salt nice, he say.  And he meant it. He's from the village on the river side of the fork. And you know, I've never been beyond the rotting Bantung tree, I told him this.  And he described every inch of the road leading to his home. It that different and that similar to ours.  He said I'd see his village as a bride.

I'll be carried to his mother's door in a four door taxi. A taxi with cool air and a radio.

I scolded him for making promises to a stranger. Then he propped my basket on his right shoulder without flinching.  "Let me carry it," he said. "You, miss, will enjoy the walk home." Issie, I walk that road everyday, but then walked it for the first time.


ISMENE: I told you not to-

ANTIGONE: Yes, I know I shouldn't have let him carry the basket,

But, how many times have I walked that road alone.


*BLACK OUT.*


## Scene 6 The Crime:


*A MAN DROPS A BASKET OF PEANUTS AT ANTIGONE'S FEET. ANTIGONE STOOPS DOWN AND SCOOPS OUT A HANDFUL OF NUTS. THE MAN TAKES A PEANUT FROM HER FINGERS, CRACKS AND POPS THE NUT INTO HIS MOUTH.*


*ANTIGONE LETS THE REMAINING PEANUTS FALL INTO THE BASKET.*


ANTIGONE: Are you tired?

MAN: Do I look so?

ANTIGONE: Yes, a little.

MAN: It's a long walk, no?

ANTIGONE: I hadn't noticed.

MAN: You make this walk everyday, then?

ANTIGONE: Yes.

MAN: I think you must be stronger than you look.

ANTIGONE: I am.

*A MOMENT.*

MAN: What's your name?

ANTIGONE: You wait until now to ask.

MAN: I wait until you're ready to tell me.

ANTIGONE: I'm not ready, but thank you mister for carrying my basket.

MAN: I'll know your name before the evening's out.

*THE SOUND OF THE NIGHT ENCROACHING.*

ANTIGONE: Well, the sky is turning over. And if you don't hurry, you won't make it home before dark.

MAN: You don't think so?


ANTIGONE: No.


*THEY BOTH GAZE UPWARD, THEN AT EACH OTHER.*


MAN: I should go then.


ANTIGONE: Yes.


*HE DOES NOT MOVE. THEY STAND FACING EACH OTHER. THEY BOTH TAKE A STEP FORWARD, BRINGING THEM CLOSER TOGETHER.*


ANTIGONE: Are you thirsty?

MAN: Your husband won't mind if you bring me a glass of water?

ANTIGONE: My husband is dead.

*A MOMENT.*

MAN: Yes, I am thirsty.

ANTIGONE: Then I'll fetch you some water.

MAN: Wait.

ANTIGONE: Yes.

MAN: I want to look at you before the light is gone.

*THE MAN STUDIES ANTIGONE. SHE STANDS
SELF-CONSCIOUSLY.*

ANTIGONE: Please. Stop. You're making me feel
silly.

MAN: I don't mean to. But I may look?

ANTIGONE: Yes.

MAN: I've been meaning to speak to you since --

ANTIGONE: I know. The windy day.

MAN: Yes, how…yes.

*THE MAN TENDERLY TAKES ANTIGONE'S
HAND. THEY STAND HOLDING HANDS.*

*ANTIGONE, AT FIRST ILL AT EASE, FINALLY ALLOWS HERSELF A SMILE.*

MAN: *(SOOTHING)* A sweet smile.

ANTIGONE: Don't say that.

MAN: It's true.

*ANTIGONE PULLS AWAY HER HAND.*

ANTIGONE: Please, go.

MAN: I'm still thirsty. And you said you'd fetch me some water.

ANTIGONE: Understand, my father's demands are large. I am a widow.

MAN: Well, I have nothing.

ANTIGONE: Then why carry my basket five miles?

MAN: To know you, maybe.

ANTIGONE: And what will be said?

MAN: Let it be said!

ANTIGONE: No.

*THE MAN GENTLY STROKES ANTIGONE'S FACE. ALARMED, ANTIGONE DRAWS BACK. HER EYES DART FROM SIDE TO SIDE, CHECKING TO SEE IF ANYONE IS LOOKING.*

MAN: We are alone.

ANTIGONE: We're not alone.  I live in this compound with my family, so I must remain nameless.  And us standing here is forbid—

MAN: Shhh.

*THE MAN TOUCHES ANTIGONE'S LIPS.*

We've done nothing that'll bring God's wrath.

ANTIGONE: It is not God that worries me.

*THE MAN MOVES IN AS TO KISS ANTIGONE, BUT SHE PULLS AWAY.*

ANTIGONE: Why won't you go?

MAN: Because if I go.  I'll see you at the market, and you won't know me.  You will look through me to the next customer. Am I right?

ANTIGONE: I can't know you.

*A MOMENT.*

I'm not the sort of woman that you think.

MAN: I carried your basket five miles and you think me that sort of man?

ANTIGONE: ...No, but--

MAN: Miss, I don't know why I'm still standing here.  But I am. I'm a simple man, a poor man from a village with nothing to recommend it. I'm a good farmer with arid land; that is me today.  But it may rain tomorrow and everything will be different... Or it may not rain for a year and I'll continue to sift dust for a family. I'll have to walk past you at the marketplace and shut my eyes. Miss, it may take me a year, I think so, to properly woo you away from your family. To earn the right to stand here by law. One long year. I'm telling you this, because I stand here disgracefully and hopefully wanting desperately to know your name. And I'll walk away now and work a year for your dowry, if that is what you want. But it is too long to wait for one kiss.

*A MOMENT.*

So if you tell me again to go, I will, because I will.

*ANOTHER MOMENT. ANTIGONE WRESTLES WITH HER UNCERTAINTY.*

*THE MAN TAKES A STEP TOWARD HER. SHE TAKES A STEP TOWARD HIM.*

ANTIGONE: I'm going to say this, and I know it will have consequences.

My name is Antigone.

MAN: Antigone.

ANTIGONE: Yes.

MAN: Why did you tell me?

ANTIGONE: Because…I like you.

MAN: I like you, too.

*THEY KISS. IT IS A RELEASE.  IT IS
PASSIONATE. AS LIGHTS SLOWLY FADE A
CHORUS OF REPORTERS VOICES RISES. WHITE
HOT FLASH BULBS.*

*A CHORUS OF REPORTERS VOICES (O.S.
AMPLIFIED)*

Did you?

Were you?

Are you aware of the law?

What would God say?

Did you?

Were you?

Do you respect the code of the law?

The law? What about the law?

# RED AGAIN

## by Chiori Miyagawa

*ANTIGONE AND HAROLD FIND THEMSELVES
IN BEAUTIFUL BLUE LIGHTS. THERE ARE
PILES OF BOOKS AROUND AND NOTHING
ELSE. A PORTION OF DOWNSTAGE REMAINS
DARK.*

ANTIGONE: *(DISORIENTED)* Harold. Where are we?

HAROLD: The underworld, I assume.

ANTIGONE: The underworld. Then you followed me here.

HAROLD: It was my destiny.

ANTIGONE: We didn't say good bye, did we?

HAROLD: I wouldn't have expected anything so sentimental from you, Antigone.

ANTIGONE: You could have lived.

HAROLD: I didn't.

ANTIGONE: I'm sorry.

HAROLD: For what?

ANTIGONE: For bringing tragedy into your life.

HAROLD: I don't mind tragedy.

ANTIGONE: I had to do what I did. Something colossal went wrong and it was changing the composition of human decency.


HAROLD: I know.


ANTIGONE: The rich grew greedier and greedier with suspicion and destruction and the poor stood mute. The earth was mutilated, animals tortured and discarded, rivers poisoned. People began to disappear. I had to bury my brother's body. I couldn't just let him disappear. He was my last brother.


HAROLD: Antigone. I don't mind tragedy. You did the right thing.


ANTIGONE: It was the right thing to do. I had to be courageous.


HAROLD: You were courageous.

ANTIGONE: The end was dark and cold. A long time passed, or no time at all. Time stopped. I was afraid of death.

HAROLD: Didn't you know that I would follow you?

ANTIGONE: I was afraid to die.

HAROLD: Now I'm here with you.

ANTIGONE: Yes. I'm no longer afraid.

*PAUSE.*

ANTIGONE: I didn't expect the underworld to be so serene. I thought I would see my doomed family.

HAROLD: This may be Bardo. A transition place.

ANTIGONE: It's rather beautiful.

HAROLD: It reminds me of the ocean. The air smells salty too.

*PAUSE.*

ANTIGONE: What would you have preferred to this?

HAROLD: Nothing. I prefer you to everything. But if you weren't so enraged all the time about the injustices of the world, I would've been happy just meditating.

ANTIGONE: You can't change the world by meditating.

HAROLD: You're wrong.


ANTIGONE: How?


HAROLD: It's too complex to explain right now.


ANTIGONE: I think we have a lot of time.


HAROLD: The point is, I knew the fire in you was irreconcilable. You were born with that fire. I didn't try to change you.


ANTIGONE: I tried to change you, didn't I? But I couldn't find a revolution that I could sign us both up for.


HAROLD: So you left me.


ANTIGONE: Because the society had gone intolerably wrong and you were still meditating. Not burying my brother, the un-patriot, would have meant that I consented to surrendering my rights to perform rituals and honor my ancestors. What would we have lost next? Freedom of speech and thought? The right not to reproduce? The right to eat meat or not to eat meat? Freedom to go roller skating?

HAROLD: Antigone, you did the right thing.

ANTIGONE: Yes, I did.

*PAUSE.*

HAROLD: After you were executed,

ANTIGONE: I wasn't. I hanged myself.

HAROLD: After you hanged yourself...I tried to kill the King. I failed.

*PAUSE.*

ANTIGONE: Thank you for following me. I was desperately lonely.

HAROLD: We were engaged. I'm keeping my promise.

*PAUSE.*

ANTIGONE: What now?

HAROLD: We wait.

*FROM THE DARK SIDE OF THE STAGE, A BLOOD CURDLING SCREAM IS HEARD. A STARK LIGHT COMES UP ON IRENE, FACING THE AUDIENCE. IRENE IS IN THE WORLD OF THE LIVING. HAROLD AND ANTIGONE FREEZE.*

IRENE: I'm reporting a double suicide. My sister Antigone hanged herself, and her boyfriend Harold found her body and then stabbed himself. My name is Irene. I live in Manhattan. Please hurry. We are being evacuated. All people of Japanese descent received notice to relocate in forty-eight hours. I'm packing my life into two suitcases that I can carry. I can't carry two dead bodies. I can't carry my sister. I can't carry her. I have to carry linen and silver and our family curse. Antigone is dead. Forever. I can't carry any more. I'm being sent far far away from home. Somewhere called Treblinka. Do you know where it is? I think it's in Bosnia. Or Cambodia. Please. I need help. I'm reporting a broken heart, broken bodies, broken humanity.

*IRENE FREEZES.*

*IN THE BLUE LIGHT, ANTIGONE SHIVERS.*

HAROLD: Are you cold?

ANTIGONE: What are we waiting for?

HAROLD: An opportunity for reincarnation.

ANTIGONE: I don't want to go back. Leaving was an immense effort. Leaving my little sister was as excruciating as the thought of continuing to live without dignity. After Polynices' death, I could not reconcile the two planes of my existence – my critical stance of the kingdom and my love for you and Irene. I didn't think personal love was enough when I no longer trusted humanity.

HAROLD: It was enough for me. The world didn't have to be larger than the people I loved. Until you were taken away from me. Then the world became painfully enormous.

ANTIGONE: Why do you want to go back?

HAROLD: We didn't get to finish our story.

ANTIGONE: Will you touch my face?

*HE DOES.*

ANTIGONE: I like it when you touch my face.

*ANTIGONE AND HAROLD FREEZE.*

IRENE: Yes, you might have called my brother
dark-skinned; though not really dark, but
definitely not creamy white. That did not make
him a terrorist. He didn't have any weapons. All
he had was a wallet which transformed into the
shape of a gun in the presence of police officers.
But I'm not calling about Polynices. Children are
being murdered everywhere by fictitious weapons
of mass destruction and economic sanctions and
post war deprivations and words like "axis of
evil." Please help. I'm calling on August 5th, 8:15
a.m.. The mushroom cloud from Hiroshima is
choking Manhattan. It's April 22, and the mustard
gas released at the eastern front of France is
choking Manhattan. It's September 11th, 8:46 a.m.
I'm reporting a broken city. Antigone and Harold
are both dead.

*IRENE FREEZES AGAIN.*

*ANTIGONE READS ONE OF THE BOOKS FROM THE PILE.*

ANTIGONE: Harold, look at this book. I know the woman in the story. I went to school with her. She married a doctor and had a life of suburban luxury, but one day, she woke up screaming. She walked right out the door of her big white house screaming, through the garden full of roses and geraniums, and became an artist. It's all in here.

HAROLD: What was her name?

ANTIGONE: Kate.

HAROLD: You've never talked about her before.

ANTIGONE: I lost touch with her after school. I often wondered what became of her.

HAROLD: What does the book say?


*ANTIGONE FLIPS THE BOOK TO THE END.*


ANTIGONE: The book is not finished. There are blank pages at the end. Kate lives in Germany. She hears about my death in the news and remembers me. Remembers that I was not so wild with rage back then. She is sad for me.


HAROLD: Look Antigone. Here is your book.


ANTIGONE: Mine?


HAROLD: Here are some things you said to the King that got you in trouble.


"I do not think your edict has such force that you, one man, can override the great, written, unshakable traditions."

"Your moralizing repels me; every word you say is a greedy lie. The public's lips are locked in fear of the ruthless power that can randomly accuse anyone of being a traitor for any reason."

ANTIGONE: I spoke the truth.

HAROLD: You sure did. I was proud of you. But the truth doesn't always equal victory. Here is the fight you and Irene had.

*AS HAROLD CONTINUES TO READ, WE SEE THE PAST REENACTED BY ANTIGONE AND IRENE, BREAKING THE INVISIBLE WALL BETWEEN THEM.*

ANTIGONE: How can you bear to leave our brother disgraced?

IRENE: They are watching us every minute. Our phone is tapped, our e-mails are scrutinized, our activities are photographed.

ANTIGONE: You didn't answer my question.

IRENE: Have we not had enough tragedy in our family? Have we not been persecuted enough? Please, let's hold onto what is left of us.

ANTIGONE: You will always know your own compromise. You will have to live with that knowledge for the rest of your life.

IRENE: Yes. I'll live to regret it. But you won't, because you'll be dead.

ANTIGONE: I won't submit to an unreasonable authority. There are certain things that are true about being human, no matter who rules us. We have the right to bury our own brother.

IRENE: We have the right to live.  Some things are bigger than you.  There is a time to wait and a time to act.  You must be patient.

ANTIGONE: Waiting and keeping silent only degrade one's soul.  You are a coward.

IRENE: Lack of survival instinct is insanity.  You are a madwoman.

ANTIGONE: I will bury him myself.

IRENE: No, Antigone.  Live.  Live with me.

ANTIGONE: You are no longer my blood.

*END OF MEMORY.  HAROLD STOPS READING.*

HAROLD: You are severe.

ANTIGONE: Poor Irene.  She is left alone with everyone's grief.   Let's not excavate tragedy anymore.


*HAROLD HANDS ANTIGONE HER BOOK AND PICKS UP HIS OWN AND OPENS IT.*


HAROLD: Here are things I said about you: Softness, intelligence, poetry, stubbornness.


*ANTIGONE LOOKS IN HER BOOK.*


ANTIGONE: Here are things I said about you: Light, humor, beauty, talks too much.


HAROLD: I stopped talking so much since I met you because you talk constantly.

ANTIGONE: Here are some other things: Tendency toward behavior commonly considered manly.

HAROLD: Chivalrous.

ANTIGONE: Tendency to claim that you know everything.

HAROLD: I know more than you do. Tendency toward occasional hysteria.

ANTIGONE: Tendency toward occasional political incorrectness. Like telling a woman she has hysteria.

HAROLD: Tendency to point out everything that is ever so slightly wrong.

ANTIGONE: Will you touch my face?

*HE DOES.*

ANTIGONE: I like it when you touch my face.

*ANTIGONE AND HAROLD FREEZE.*

IRENE: Yes, I've called a few times before. My
family was dysfunctional. Yes, Oedipus, who
gouged his own eyes out for his crimes of
unnatural sex and patricide, was my father.
Jocasta, who hanged herself, was both his wife
and his mother. And my mother. My two brothers
Eteocles and Polynices, born of incest, died at each
other's hand. Yes, I called the ambulance service
each time. I'm still entitled to police assistance.
I'm an American citizen.

Antigone and Harold each left a note. What do
you mean that you know the contents already? I
have them here. The notes are addressed to me.
These were the last private and intimate words of
the last two people who cared about me. How did

you get them?  They weren't even mailed.  They were left on my bedside table.

You are not sending any help, are you?  I'm on my own with two corpses.  You are busy because it's nearly dawn on April 30th, and the last Marines in Saigon are lifting off.  It's January 17th 2:38 am, and the air strike over Baghdad has begun…

*IRENE BREAKS FROM ADDRESSING THE AUDIENCE.*

*(DISTRAUGHT)* Antigone, Antigone, my sister,

*ANTIGONE HEARS IRENE FOR THE FIRST TIME.*

ANTIGONE: Irene?

*IRENE DOES NOT HEAR ANTIGONE.*

IRENE: You shouldn't have chosen death. There are things to live for. There is always something to live for. Even here in Rwanda during the civil war, no, I mean during Ethnic Cleansing. No, that's not right either. Afghanistan? No. Even here in occupied Manchuria. What? What do I have to live for? Oh, Antigone, I am so alone. So completely alone. So unnaturally alone.

ANTIGONE: Irene, Irene. Can you hear me? I want to tell you about the books I found in the underworld. Each person has a book, and as one lives life, her story gets recorded in the book. I looked in your book. You have many blank pages still. Your story continues.

IRENE: You were right. The damage done to human decency, democracy, and rational thinking is too great. There is no turning back. We live in lies and racial profiling and threats disguised as freedom speeches, and no one will help me bury your paleness and Harold's bloody red. The city is under high security alert, the color Red. Red City. Red in my house. Red human history.

ANTIGONE: No, Irene. These books. I found the books of human effort. There are more books here. Completely blank ones for new lives.

IRENE: They read yours and Harold's notes. So now I have nothing. Nothing is mine. They own my memories.

*DURING ANTIGONE'S NEXT SPEECH, LIGHTS FADE ON IRENE.*

ANTIGONE: I know right now it feels like all violent acts and atrocities in human history are converging and happening in one instant. I know it feels like that instant is a loop and it plays and plays and never stops. Red, again and again. But there is white in these books. Irene, please hear me.

HAROLD: Antigone, Irene will survive. You always thought you were the stronger one, but in the end, the strongest lives. She lives.

ANTIGONE: I wrote in my note to her that I had no choice but to leave her; I had to be brave.

HAROLD: I wrote to her that I was following you because otherwise you'd be afraid.

ANTIGONE: Tendency to divulge unnecessary information.

HAROLD: Tendency toward bravado.  Gets us killed every time.

*PAUSE*

HAROLD: I found two blank books.  One cover says "former Harold" and the other says "former Antigone."  We are going back.

ANTIGONE: Going back to Red again.

HAROLD: We have work to do.

ANTIGONE: Will we find each other?

HAROLD: It's our destiny.

ANTIGONE: You should look for me fighting in a revolution.

HAROLD: Look for me meditating in a monastery.

ANTIGONE: Did you really try to kill the King?

HAROLD: It was a pathetic attempt. But I spat at him at least.

ANTIGONE: We won't remember each other, will we?

HAROLD: Not initially.  But before the end of our story, we will love each other again.

ANTIGONE: Yes, I'm no longer afraid.

Harold

I follow you.

*THEY LOOK INTO EACH OTHER'S EYES AND THEN LOOK TO THE AUDIENCE.*

*BLUE LIGHTS FADE.*

**END OF PLAY,  ANTIGONE PROJECT**

*Red Again* by Chiori Miyagawa, Directed by
Barbara Rubin

@ The Women's Project, 2004, photo: T. Charles
Erickson.

# Biographies

**TANYA BARFIELD**'s plays include: *Of Equal Measure* (Center Theatre Group), *Blue Door* (Playwrights Horizons, South Coast Repertory; Seattle Repertory, Berkeley Repertory, Harare International Festival of the Arts, Zimbabwe), *Dent, The Quick, The Houdini Act* and *121º West*. Short plays include *Foul Play* (Royal Court Theatre, Cultural Center Bank of Brazil), *The Wolves* and *Wanting North* (Guthrie Theatre Lab, published in: Best 10-Minute Plays of 2003). She wrote the book for the Theatreworks/USA children's musical, *Civil War: The First Black Regiment* which has toured public schools around the country. She was a recipient of the 2003 Helen Merrill Award for Emerging Playwrights, 2005 Honorable Mention for the Kesselring Prize for Drama, a 2006 Lark Play Development/NYSCA grant and she has been twice been a Finalist for the Princess Grace Award. She has been commissioned by Playwrights Horizons, Center

Theatre Group, South Coast Repertory, Primary Stages and Geva Theatre Center. Tanya was an invited guest to the "Legacy" Tribute Dinner to the Civil Rights Generation on Capitol. She is a Resident Playwright at New Dramatists.

**KAREN HARTMAN** is an award-winning playwright and librettist whose work has been supported by the Rockefeller Foundation, the N.E.A., the Helen Merrill Foundation, a Daryl Roth "Creative Spirit" Award, a Hodder Fellowship, a Jerome Fellowship, a Fulbright Scholarship to Jerusalem, a New Dramatists residency, and Core Membership at the Playwrights Center. Her plays, *Goldie, Max, and Milk; Goliath; Donna Wants; Gum; Going Gone; Anatomy 1968; Troy Women; ALICE: Tales of a Curious Girl; Leah's Train* and others have been commissioned and/or staged by dozens of theaters including the Women's Project, NAATCO, McCarter Theater, ACT in San Francisco, Center Stage, the Magic Theater, and Dallas Theater Center, and are published by TCG, DPS, Backstage Books, and Playscripts. Musical projects include the book for *Sea Change*, score by AnnMarie Milazzo, directed by Leigh Silverman. Karen holds a B.A. from Yale University and an M.F.A. from the Yale School of Drama. She has taught playwriting in a wide range of settings including four years at the Yale School of Drama.

CHIORI MIYAGAWA is a Japanese-born, American playwright. Her plays include *America Dreaming*, commissioned by Music-Theatre Group, directed by Michael Mayer at Vineyard Theatre (published in Global Foreigners Seagull Books); *Nothing Forever* and *Yesterday's Window* (both at New York Theatre Workshop, directed by Karin Coonrod, *Nothing* published in Positive/Negative Women, *Yesterday* published in TAKE TEN), *Woman Killer* (Crossing Jamaica Avenue in co-production with HERE, published in Plays and Playwrights 2002), *Leaving Eden* (The Meadows School of the Arts, SMU Commission, directed by Greg Leaming), *Jamaica Avenue* (New York International Fringe Festival, published in Tokens? The NYC Asian American Experiences on Stage), *FireDance* (Voice&Vision), *Broken Morning* (Dallas Theater Center and Crossing Jamaica Avenue in co-production with HERE), *Antigone's Red* (Virginia Tech, published in TAKE TEN II.) A collection of her plays, *Thousand Years Waiting and Other Plays*, is forthcoming from Seagull Books as part of the international play series, *In Performance*, for which Carol Martin is the general editor. Chiori has been awarded many grants and fellowships including the New York Foundation for the Arts Playwriting Fellowship,

McKnight Playwriting Fellowship, Van Lier Playwriting Fellowship, and Asian Cultural Council Fellowship Rockefeller Bellagio Residency, and Radcliffe Advanced Studies Fellowship at Harvard University.

**LYNN NOTTAGE** is the author of *Ruined*, which received the 2009 Pulitzer Prize for Drama, and was produced at the Goodman Theatre in Chicago and at the Manhattan Theatre Club. Her play *Intimate Apparel*, which was produced at the Roundabout Theatre Company and received the 2004 New York Drama Critics' Circle Award for Best Play. *Fabulation, or the Education of Undine*, was produced by Playwrights Horizons and at the Tricycle Theatre in London. Her most recent play is  Her other plays include *Crumbs from the Table of Joy; Las Meninas; Mud, River, Stone; Por'Knockers* and *Poof!* She is the recipient of the 2004 PEN/Laura Pels Award, the 2005 Guggenheim grant for playwriting, and fellowships from Manhattan Theatre Club, New Dramatists and the New York Foundation for the Arts. She is an alumna of New Dramatists, a recipient of the MacArthur Foundation "Genius Grant" Award, and a graduate of Brown University and the Yale School of Drama.

**CARIDAD SVICH** is a US Latina playwright, translator, lyricist and editor whose works have been presented across the US and abroad at diverse venues including The Women's Project, INTAR, 59East59, Theater for the New City, Repertorio Espanol, McCarren Park Pool, Walkerspace, 7 Stages, Salvage Vanguard Theatre, ARTheater-Cologne, and Edinburgh Fringe Festival/UK. Among her key works: *12 Ophelias, Any Place But Here, Alchemy of Desire/Dead-Man's Blues, Fugitive Pieces, Instructions for Breathing, Iphigenia...a rave fable, The House of the Spirits* (based on the Allende novel), *The Tropic of X, The Booth Variations* and *Wreckage.* She has translated nearly all of Federico Garcia Lorca's plays as well as works by Lope de Vega, Calderon de la Barca, Julio Cortazar and new plays from Spain, Cuba and Mexico and has adapted works by Wedekind, Sophocles, Euripides and Shakespeare. She is alumna playwright of New Dramatists, founder of theatre alliance & press NoPassport, associate editor of Routledge's *Contemporary Theatre Review* and contributing editor of *TheatreForum.* She's been a Radcliffe Institute for Advanced Studies Fellow at Harvard University's, and is member of PEN American Center, The Dramatists Guild and is featured in the <u>Oxford Encyclopedia of Latino</u>

History. She holds an MFA from UCSD. She's taught playwriting at Bard College, UCSD, Bennington College, Ohio State University, Denison University and the Yale School of Drama. Website: www.caridadsvich.com

For the *Antigone Project:*

**SABRINA PECK** (Co-Conceiver) conceives and directs original theater works infused with movement and music, often in collaboration with diverse communities. Productions include *Common Green/Common Ground*, with community gardeners in NYC; *Odakle Ste* with Bosnian Muslim refugees in Croatia; and *Commodities*, with commodities pit traders on Wall Street. Peck has also helped to develop the work of playwrights, directing productions or staged readings at Dance Theater Workshop, New Dramatists, New Georges, The New World Theater, The Public Theater and The Vineyard Theater. She has choreographed for Lincoln Center Theater, Yale Repertory Theatre, The New York Shakespeare Festival and others. Peck has taught at NYU Tisch School of the Arts and Duke University, and was the Peter Ivers Visiting Artist at Harvard

University. She is a longtime Associate Artist with Cornerstone Theater Company. Her work is detailed in the books, *Local Acts: Community-Based Performance in the United States* by Jan Cohen-Cruz and *Staging America: Cornerstone and Community-Based Theater* by Sonja Kuftinec. Portfolio: www.sabrinapeck.com

For this volume:

**MARIANNE MCDONALD** (Introduction) is a Professor of Theatre and Classics at the University of California, San Diego. She was a Fulbright professor in 1999, is adjunct professor at Trinity College Dublin, a fellow at the National University of Ireland and is one of the few women to have been elected a member of the Royal Irish Academy. Professor McDonald was trained in classics and music and taught for many years at the University of California, Irvine. She is most well-known for her work on ancient Greek drama, mythology, and modern versions of ancient classics in film, plays and opera, but her poems, plays, and translations have also been widely published. A dedicated teacher and international lecturer, she is a pioneer in the field of modern versions of the classics, in the films, plays and opera. She has over 200 publications. Website: www.mmcdonald.info.


**LISA SCHLESINGER** (Preface)'s plays include *Wal-martyrs, Celestial Bodies, Twenty-One Positions* (with Naomi Wallace and Abed Abu Srour), *Same Egg, Manny and Chicken* and *Harmonicus Mundi*, an opera. She has received commissions from the Guthrie Theatre, the BBC, Portland Stage Company and fellowships from the NEA, CEC International and the Sloan Foundation. She is winner of the BBC International Playwriting Award. She is Professor of Playwriting at Columbia College Chicago

# NoPassport

**NoPassport** is a Pan-American theatre alliance & press devoted to live, virtual and print action, advocacy and change toward the fostering of cross-cultural diversity in the arts with an emphasis on the embrace of the hemispheric spirit in US Latina/o and Latin-American theatre-making. **NoPassport Press'** Dreaming the Americas Series and Theatre & Performance PlayTexts Series promotes new writing for the stage, texts on theory and practice and theatrical translations.

### Series Editors:

Jorge Huerta, Otis Ramsey-Zoe, Caridad Svich

### Advisory Board:

Daniel Banks, Amparo Garcia-Crow, Maria M. Delgado, Randy Gener, Elana Greenfield, Christina Marin, Antonio Ocampo Guzman, Sarah Cameron Sunde, Saviana Stanescu, Tamara Underiner, Patricia Ybarra